FIREMAN

AND THE BOAT RESCUE

story by Rob Lee
illustrations by the County Studio

HEINEMANN · LONDON

It had been raining non-stop for days in Pontypandy. Station Officer Steele called Fireman Sam and Elvis Cridlington together.

"There's been an official flood warning," said Station Officer Steele. "We must get sandbags loaded and delivered as quickly as possible!"

"Righto, Sir!" replied Sam.

Sam and Elvis loaded Jupiter's lockers with sandbags.
"Phew! They weigh a ton!" puffed Elvis. "But at least we'll
have an appetite for my Hungarian beetroot stew."

"Sounds about as tasty as these sandbags," muttered Sam.

Station Officer Steele decided to arrange for the boats at
Pontypandy boating lake to be put on standby.

The twins were in Bella's café drinking lemonade when Fireman Sam and Elvis arrived carrying sandbags.

"Hi, Uncle Sam!" called Sarah and James.

"Whatever have you got there?" asked Bella.

"Sandbags!" replied Elvis.

"There's been a flood warning," said Fireman Sam. "These bags will give you extra protection."

Bella still looked baffled. "Don't worry," chuckled Sam. "They're not for making sandcastles! You put them at the bottom of your doors to keep the water out."

Over tea, Fireman Sam explained to Bella what to do in a flood.

"Make sure you've got a good torch handy," said Sam. "It's a good idea to switch the electricity off at the mains."

Bella was so busy listening to Sam that she didn't notice her cat Rosa slip out of the front door.

Soon afterwards, Fireman Sam and Elvis called at Dilys
Price's shop to deliver the sandbags. They were astonished
when they walked inside. The shelves were absolutely bare!

"Where's all your stock?" asked Fireman Sam.

"H-have you been robbed?" gulped Elvis.

"No! I heard about the flood so I've moved my stock
upstairs," chuckled Dilys.

"Well, that's sensible," laughed Fireman Sam. "But I don't
think the water's going to be quite that high!"

"It doesn't pay to take chances," sniffed Dilys in reply.

Later at the station a message came through.
Station Officer Steele looked at it carefully, then called out to Fireman Sam and Elvis. "Jump to it lads! Pandy River has burst its banks."

"Great fires of London!" cried Sam. "Man the boats!"

Station Officer Steele, Fireman Sam and Elvis climbed into Jupiter and sped through the rain to the boating lake.

As they arrived in Pontypandy, the rain stopped, but the town was already flooded with water from the river. Bella and the twins gazed out of the café window as it almost lapped up to the window ledge.

"There's Uncle Sam!" cried James as Fireman Sam rowed his boat through the town, closely followed by Station Officer Steele and Elvis rowing a boat full of animal feed.

"I'd better get Sarah and James home," called Fireman Sam.

"I'll head out to Pandy Farm," replied Station Officer
Steele, "in case there are any animals stranded by the flood."

Fireman Sam rowed up to the side window of Bella's café
and helped the twins into the boat. The twins giggled with
excitement.

"I can't find Rosa!" called Bella. "Can you keep an eye out
for her, Sam?"

"Will do," replied Fireman Sam.

"Look, there's Norman, Sir!" cried Elvis, as they rowed through Pontypandy Park.

Norman Price was stranded on top of the bandstand.

"What on earth are you doing up there?" asked Station Officer Steele.

"I didn't want to get my trainers wet," replied Norman. He leapt into the boat, almost capsizing it.

"Whoaah!" cried Elvis.

"Landlubber!" muttered Station Officer Steele.

By now, Fireman Sam had dropped off Sarah and James. Suddenly he spotted Trevor sitting on the roof of his bus.

"What's happened?" asked Fireman Sam. "Has your engine seized up?"

"Yes," replied Trevor. "Thank goodness you've arrived. I thought I'd starve to death up here!"

"It's not even lunchtime yet!" chuckled Fireman Sam. Trevor climbed into the boat nervously.

"Easy does it," said Fireman Sam as he helped Trevor into his seat.

"I hope I don't get seasick!" muttered Trevor.

"I hope not, too," laughed Fireman Sam. "We'll need your services as an auxiliary fireman today." Fireman Sam was heading back to the station when Trevor remembered he had a delivery for Bella aboard his bus.

"Don't worry," said Fireman Sam. "The café won't be open today, that's for sure."

Meanwhile Station Officer Steele, Elvis and Norman had reached Pandy Farm.

"Look!" cried Norman getting to his feet. "There's some sheep!"

Elvis rowed towards the stranded sheep. "Starboard a bit…" Station Officer Steele ordered, "… a little bit to port!"

"We'll never get all those sheep on board!" said Norman.

"Silly boy," replied Station Officer Steele. "We'll just leave them enough feed to last until the flood subsides."

"Elvis," said Norman, "can I have a go at rowing please?"

Elvis didn't look too sure, but handed over the oars to Norman.

"It's not as easy as it looks," said Station Officer Steele as Norman prepared to pull the first stroke.

"Oooh, they're too heavy for me!" wailed Norman. He dropped the oars in the water.

"N-Now what?" asked Elvis as the oars disappeared.

"We'll have to paddle with our hands!" replied Station Officer Steele.

But with Elvis and Norman paddling on one side of the boat
and only Station Officer Steele on the other, the boat went
round in circles!

"Norman!" barked Station Officer Steele. "Sit with your
arms folded!"

Eventually they reached the island and scrambled out of
the boat.

Sitting on the grassy island surrounded by sheep, Norman said forlornly, "We could be stranded here for ages!"

"We could send a message in a bottle," suggested Elvis.

"Don't be silly, Cridlington!" growled Station Officer Steele. "What do you think this is for?" He pulled a two-way radio from his pocket.

"Great!" exclaimed Elvis. "You can call the station."

"Precisely," replied Steele as he pressed the call button and said, "Neptune one to Neptune two, over."

At the station, Fireman Sam and Trevor were having a mug of tea when Station Officer Steele's call came over Sam's radio handset.

Fireman Sam answered the call, "Neptune two to Neptune one, receiving you loud and clear, over."

Station Officer Steele explained the situation to Fireman Sam.

"Don't worry Neptune one, I'll come to your rescue immediately," replied Fireman Sam, trying not to laugh.

Fireman Sam went to the garage and removed a tow rope from Jupiter's locker.

"What's up?" asked Trevor.

"Station Officer Steele and Elvis are stranded," chuckled Sam. "I've got to go and rescue them."

"Do you need any help?" asked Trevor.

"No, I can manage," replied Fireman Sam. "You look after the phones."

Sam rowed through Pontypandy on the way to Pandy Farm.
"Have you seen Rosa yet, Fireman Sam?" called Bella.
"Not yet," replied Sam, "but I'll keep my eyes peeled!"

"We're saved!" shouted Norman when he spotted Fireman Sam coming towards them.

Fireman Sam pulled up alongside Station Officer Steele's boat and began tying up the tow rope.

"What happened to the oars?" asked Sam.

"A certain little stowaway made us lose them!" growled Station Officer Steele as they clambered back into their boat.

Norman gulped nervously. "I think I'll j-jump in with you, Fireman Sam."

"Not to worry," grinned Sam, "you're all safe now."

Fireman Sam called the station on his radio and told Trevor that everybody was rescued safely, then he rowed into Pontypandy High Street.

"I'd better drop you off first, Norman," said Fireman Sam. "Your mother will be worried."

As Sam pulled in at the shop, Dilys was at the window.
"My little angel!" she cried. "Thank goodness you're safe!"
"I was stranded, Mam!" cried Norman. "It was great!"
"Next time we'll leave you there!" muttered Station Officer
Steele under his breath.

Two days later, it was bright and sunny and the flood had gone. Fireman Sam gave Trevor a lift back to his bus.

"With a bit of luck the sun will have dried out your engine, Trevor," said Fireman Sam as they pulled over to where the bus was parked.

"I think I'd be better off with a water bus," chuckled Trevor as they climbed down.

Fireman Sam lifted the bonnet of Trevor's bus.

"It doesn't look too damp, Trev," said Fireman Sam. "Give it a try."

Trevor climbed into the driver's seat and turned the ignition key. The engine coughed and spluttered.

"Try again," called Fireman Sam.

"It's no use!" replied Trevor. "It's completely dead."

Fireman Sam got out his tool kit and worked on the engine, but it was no use.

"I'm afraid it's going to take a while to dry out, Trevor," said Fireman Sam scratching his head.

"Can you give me a tow to the garage, Sam?" asked Trevor.

"No problem," replied Fireman Sam as he made for Jupiter. Looking through the locker, he realised that he'd left his tow rope attached to the boat.

"Not to worry," said Trevor. "I've got one in the bus."

Trevor opened up the back doors and couldn't believe his eyes. Fireman Sam looked over Trevor's shoulder.

"Well, well …!" chuckled Fireman Sam.

Rosa was curled up asleep on the back seat!

Meanwhile, Bella and the twins had been searching for Rosa. They looked everywhere: in the basement, around the dustbins and up the garden tree.

"It's no use!" Bella moaned. "My poor Rosa must be lost!"

"Don't worry Bella," said Sarah soothingly. "Rosa will turn up, she always does."

"I hope she didn't come to any harm in the flood," whispered Bella, wiping away a tear.

Meanwhile, Fireman Sam had tied the tow rope from
Trevor's bus to Jupiter.

"I've done enough towing to last me a lifetime!" laughed
Fireman Sam as he climbed aboard the fire engine.

"Ready, Trevor?" called Fireman Sam.

Trevor gave the thumbs up and they drove off.

Sam steered Jupiter carefully through the winding lanes of Pontypandy as he headed for the town centre. In Trevor's bus, Rosa sat on the passenger seat calmly enjoying the view.

"Bella will be pleased to see you looking safe and sound," chuckled Trevor. "And while we're at the café, I can drop off my delivery."

Bella and the twins were outside the café when Trevor and
Fireman Sam arrived.

"I've got a surprise for you, Bella," called Trevor as he
carried Rosa off the bus.

"Rosa!" cried Bella as she gave her a big hug. "Where have
you been?"

"Snug on the back seat of Trevor's bus!" chuckled Sam.

"Poor Rosa must be starving," said Bella.

Trevor opened a wooden box he'd brought for Bella.

"I don't think she's exactly starving," said Trevor.
"My delivery to you was a box of fresh fish!" he laughed.
"Until Rosa found them!"

"During the flood Rosa was the safest, best fed cat in
Pontypandy!" cried Sam.

"Bellissima!" laughed Bella. "Come inside and I'll make
you the best fed bus driver and fireman in Pontypandy!"

FIREMAN SAM SAYS:

If you see someone in trouble in deep water, always go to an adult for help. Never try and help them yourself, even if you can swim.

William Heinemann Ltd, Michelin House
81 Fulham Road London SW3 6RB

LONDON   MELBOURNE   AUCKLAND

First published 1992 by William Heinemann Ltd
Text copyright © 1992 William Heinemann Ltd
Illustrations copyright © 1992 William Heinemann Ltd
Fireman Sam copyright © 1985 Prism Art & Design Ltd
All rights reserved
Based on the animation series produced by
Bumper Films for S4C – Channel 4 Wales –
and Prism Art & Design Ltd
Original idea by Dave Gingell and Dave Jones,
assisted by Mike Young
Characters created by Rob Lee
ISBN 434 96103 5
Printed in Italy by OFSA